For our Grammi
We love you as much as we love
doughnuts and coffee.

CDBL & Mrs. C - R.C.
Mr. K MMS - P.K.

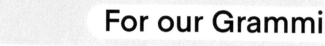

CHRIS. DOUGH. PHER.

By: Rachael Cholak & Peyton Kuryanowicz

This book belongs to:

_____

Breakfast is Christopher's favorite meal of the day.
He thinks about it nonstop.

He eats fluffy pancakes with butter
and syrup, a few crisp apples, and
so many sprinkled doughnuts.
Doughnuts are his favorite!

One morning, Christopher ate so many sprinkled doughnuts for breakfast.

He ate all of the breakfast food in the house!

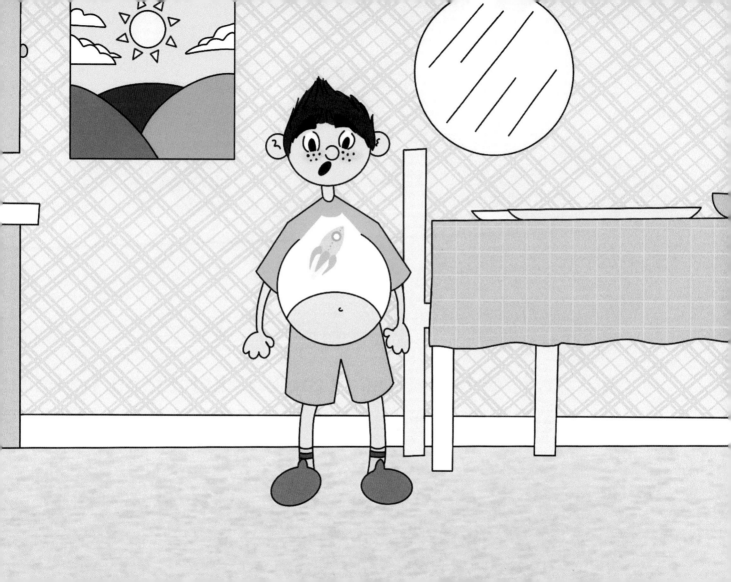

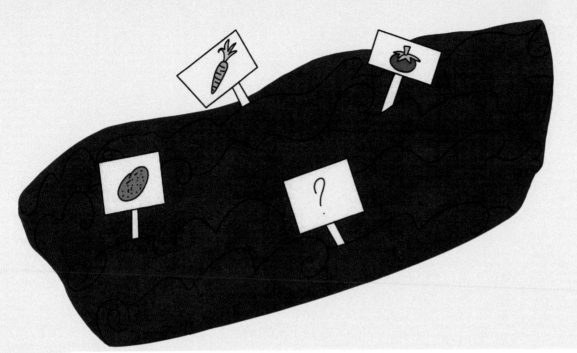

After Christopher ate all of the breakfast food, he had a great idea. He decided to grow his own food so he could eat even more.

He grew potatoes, tomatoes, carrots, and...

Suddenly, Christopher had an idea. He thought of his favorite breakfast food and wondered, "What will happen if I plant a sprinkle?" He giggled about the silly idea but still planted it.

He watered it, watched it, and waited to see.

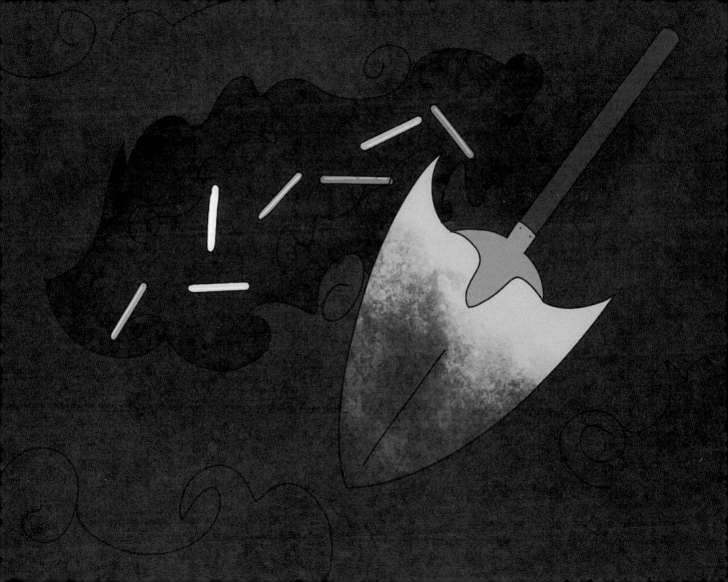

Soon, his neighbors could see that Christopher's crop was filled with tomatoes, potatoes, carrots, and... DOUGHNUTS!

They couldn't stop staring and started to drool.

But sharing was something Christopher did not like to do.

He wanted the doughnuts all to himself.

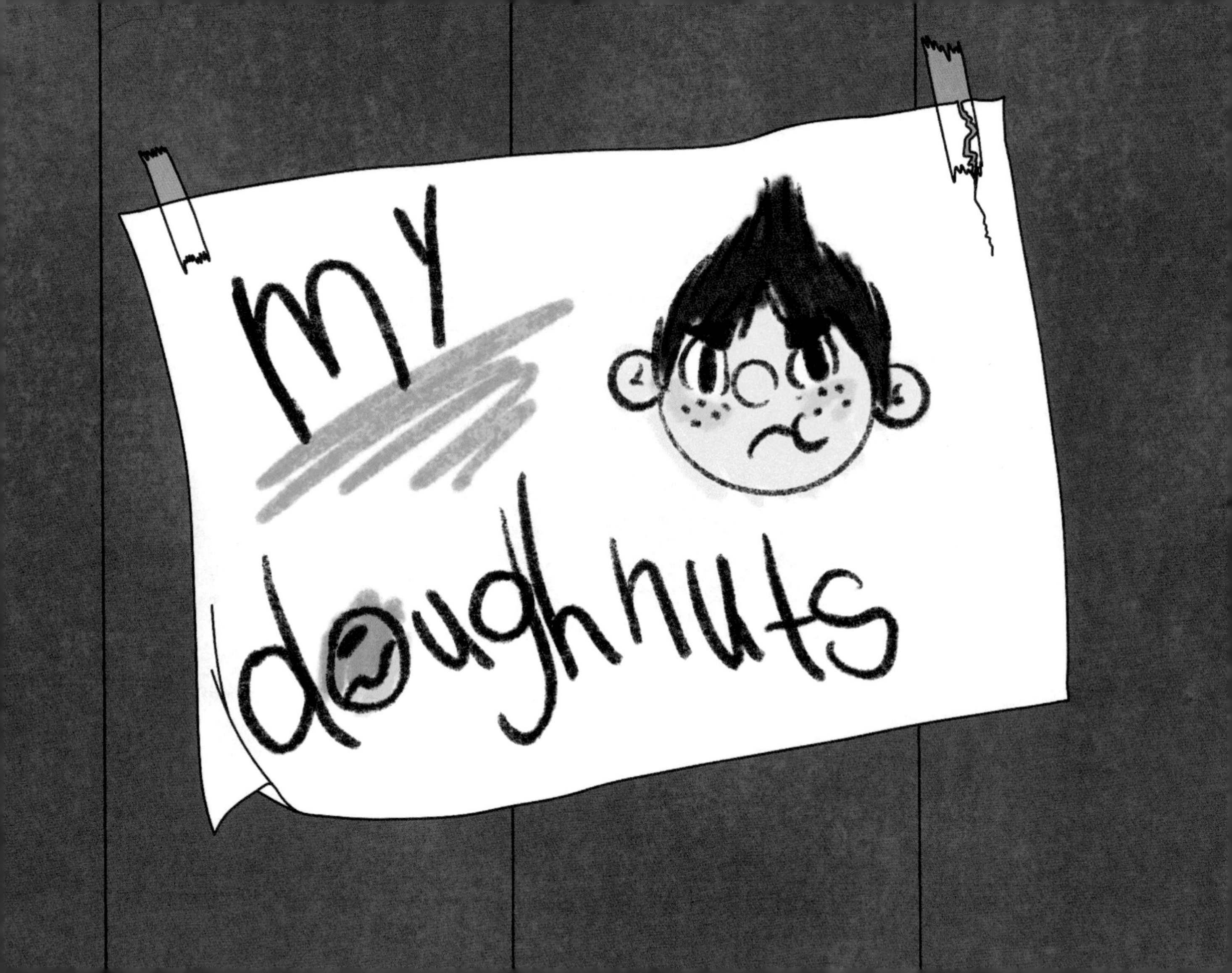
my
doughnuts

Christopher tried to eat all of the doughnuts he grew...

but he knew that the doughnuts were going to get stale soon.

To make sure that no doughnuts went to waste, Christopher decided to share with his neighbors.

He said, "Doughnuts deserve to be eaten fresh and enjoyed by all!"

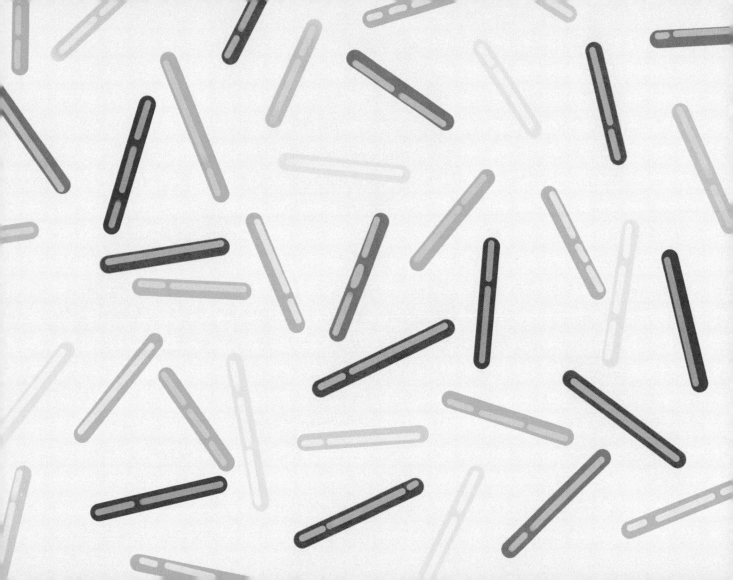

I'm sharing this book with:

_____ _____ _____

_____ _____ _____

Made in the USA
Coppell, TX
30 December 2020